Out Came the Sun

Out Came the Sun
A Day in Nursery Rhymes

Heather
Collins

KIDS CAN PRESS

Introduction

When you sing *The Eensy Weensy Spider* to your baby, bounce to the sounds of *Higglety, Pigglety, Pop* or clap hands together to *Pat-a-Cake, Pat-a-Cake*, you're not only engaging her senses, but also inspiring a love of reading. Your baby loves your voice, your touch, and is drawn to the rhythms heard and felt through your body. Babies don't need books at first — they just need you. But once you add books, you'll find that the best ones are as pleasurable for you as they are for your child. Every time children hear the words of a story or rhyme and follow the pictures, they are making connections, and if the story in the pictures is strong and can stand on its own, they will eagerly explore it — alone or with an adult. This is how a child "reads" long before he or she can actually make out the words.

In fact, your picture-reading toddler might notice what's special about this book before you do. You might think it's just another anthology of nursery rhymes, but look closely — there's so much more going on!

When I was asked to do a nursery rhyme anthology, I knew I wanted to do something different. The rhymes are carefully chosen, firstly, because they delight me and, secondly and most interestingly, because with the illustrations they work together to tell a story of a single, adventure-filled day in the lives of an endearing family of stuffed animals. They share a big, yellow house in

a countryside of rolling hills dotted with trees, charming pitched-roof cottages, a meandering stream, a little village on the hillside, sheep in the meadows and cows in the corn. From the time these cuddly characters are awakened in the morning by cock robin's song till they're finally tucked into their beds under the gaze of a kindly moon, the story rolls along, making this book a different kind of anthology altogether.

My characters' little world isn't a place any of us actually live in, but it's a place that's fun for me to imagine — a simpler place, a place that came out of the rhymes and stories I heard and the illustrations I pored over as a child, and then again as a parent with my own children. A pile of library books surrounded us on the bed each night. I introduced my childern to all my favorites and can still recall their squeals of laughter as I tickled them to *Round and Round the Garden*. I rarely resisted their pleas for one more story because I loved the time snuggled together as much as they did. I've been illustrating children's books for over thirty years, and this place, these characters and their little world come from the most comfortable and joyful part of me.

I loved working on this book, from choosing the rhymes to exploring the characters — who, yes, became "real" to me after a while! Stuffed bunnies, piglets and even spiders develop distinctive and quirky personalities when you spend so much time drawing them, painting them and tucking them into bed at night. I hope you'll delight in this book with your baby or toddler and find yourself falling in love with the rhymes — whether all over again or for the very first time.

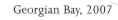

Georgian Bay, 2007

Cock robin got up early,
At the break of day,

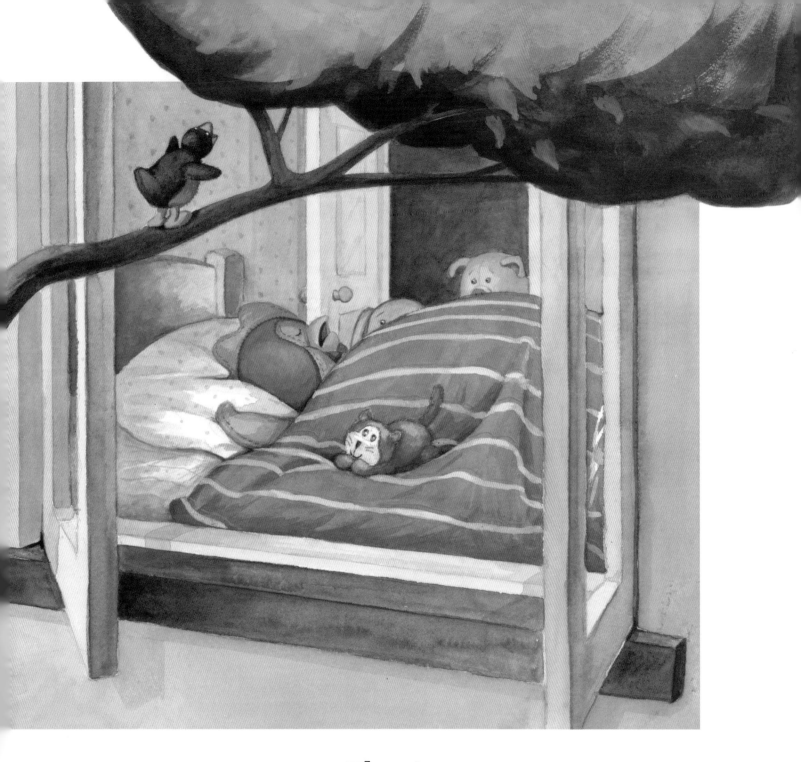

And went to Elsie's window
To sing a roundelay.

Elsie Marley's
   grown so fine,
She won't get up
   to feed the swine,
But lies in bed
   till eight or nine!
Lazy Elsie Marley.

9

I can tie my **shoelaces**,

I can brush my **hair**,

I can wash my **face** and **hands**,

And **dry** myself with care.

I can clean my **teeth**,

And fasten up my **frocks**,

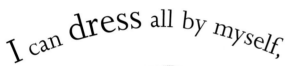

I can **dress** all by myself,

And pull up **all** my socks.

11

Rain on the green grass,
  And rain on the tree,
Rain on the housetop,

But not on ME.

13

Pease porridge hot,
　　Pease porridge cold,
Pease porridge in the pot
　　Nine days old.

Some like it hot,
　　Some like it cold,
Some like it in the pot
　　Nine days old.

Pat-a-cake, pat-a-cake,
baker's man,

Bake me a cake
as fast as you can.

Pat it and prick it,
And mark it with

B,

And put it in the oven for Baby and me.

Mix a pancake, stir a pancake, pop it in the pan.

Fry a pancake, toss a pancake, catch it if you can!

19

Jack be nimble,
Jack be quick,

Jack jump over the candlestick.

Hickory,
dickory,
dock,

The mouse
ran up
the clock.

The clock
struck one,

The mouse
ran down,

Hickory,
dickory,
dock.

Wiggle fingers,
wiggle so,

24

Wiggle **high**,

Wiggle **low**,

Wiggle **left**
and wiggle **right**,

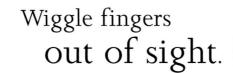

Wiggle fingers
out of sight.

25

Do your **ears** hang low?
 Do they wobble to and fro?
Can you tie them in a knot,
 Can you tie them in a bow?
Can you throw them over your shoulder,
 Like a continental soldier?

Do your **ears** hang low?

Higglety, pigglety, pop,

The dog has eaten the mop.

The pig's in a hurry, the cat's in a flurry,

Higglety, pigglety, POP!

Round about, round about,
Catch a wee mouse.
Up a bit, up a bit,
In a wee house.

30

Rain, rain, go away. Come again another day.

Rain, rain, go away. Little spider wants to play!

The eensy weensy spider
Climbed up the water spout.
Down came the rain,
And washed the spider out.

Out came the sun,
And dried up all the rain,
And the eensy weensy spider
Went up the spout again.

One, two,
Buckle my shoe,

Three, four,
Shut the door,

Five, six,
Pick up sticks,

Seven, eight,

Lay them straight,

Nine, ten,

A big red hen!

Oh where, oh where has my little dog gone?
  Oh where, oh where can he be?
With his ears cut short and his tail cut long,
  Oh where, oh where is he?

Rock-a-bye baby, in the treetop.

When the wind blows, the cradle will rock.

When the bough breaks, the cradle will fall,
And down will come baby, cradle and all.

This little cow eats grass,

This little cow eats hay,

This little cow drinks water

This little cow runs away,

And this little cow does nothing but lie around all day.

Round and round the garden, like a teddy bear.
One step,
two step,
tickle you
under there!

Teddy bear,
teddy bear,
turn around.

Teddy bear,
teddy bear,
touch the ground.

Teddy bear,
teddy bear,
tie your shoes.

Teddy bear,
teddy bear,
I love you.

45

Two little dicky birds sitting on a wall,
One named Peter, one named Paul.

Fly away, Peter, fly away, Paul,
Come back, Peter, come back, Paul.

Down by the station, early in the morning,
See the little puffer bellies all in a row.

See the stationmaster pull the little handle,
PUFF! PUFF! TOOT! TOOT! Off we go!

49

Little Miss Muffet sat on a tuffet,
Eating her curds and whey.

Along came a spider who sat down beside her,
And frightened Miss Muffet away.

Cobbler, cobbler, mend my shoe,
Get it done by half past two.
Cobbler, cobbler, mend my shoe,
'Cause my toe is **peeping** through.

Baa, baa, black sheep,
Have you any wool?

Yes sir, yes sir,
Three bags full.

One for the master,

One for the dame,

And **one** for the little boy
Who lives down the lane.

To market, to market,
To find a fat pig,
Home again, home again,
Jiggety-jig.

To market, to market,
To find a fat hog,
Home again, home again,
Jiggety-jog.

Dickory, dickory, dare,
The pig flew up in the air.

A bird in brown soon brought him down,
Dickory, dickory, dare.

Little Fee Wee,

He went to sea

In an open boat.

And while afloat,
The little boat bended —
My story's ended.

Little boy blue,
  Come blow your horn,
The sheep's in the meadow,
  The cow's in the corn.

Where is the girl
  Who looks after the sheep?
She's under a haystack fast asleep.

Little Bo-Peep has lost her sheep,
And doesn't know where to find them.
Leave them alone, and they'll come home,
Wagging their tails behind them.

The hen's in the house
blowing her horn,
The COW'S in the barn
thrashing the corn,

The **sheep's** in the meadow
making hay,
And the **duck's** in the river
swimming away.

Jack and Jill went up the hill to fetch a pail of water,

Jack fell down and broke his crown, and Jill came tumbling after.

Elsie put the kettle on, kettle on, kettle on,
Elsie put the kettle on, and we'll all have tea.

Quickly take it off again, off again, off again,
Quickly take it off again, they've all gone away.

Here's a cup,
And here's a cup,
And here's a pot of tea.

Pour a cup,
And pour a cup,
And have a drink with me.

I'm a little **teapot**,
Short
and
stout.

Here is my handle,
Here is my spout.

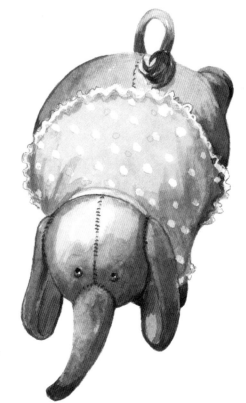

When I get all steamed up,
Hear me **shout**,

Tip me over
And pour me **out**.

73

Who made the pie?
I did!

Who stole the pie?
He did!

Who found the pie?
She did!

Who ate the pie?
You did!

Who cried for the pie? They ALL did!

I saw you in the orchard,
I saw you in the sea.

I saw you in the bathtub,

Whoops! Pardon me.

Wee Willie Winkie
  Runs through the town,
Upstairs and downstairs
  In his nightgown,
Rapping on the window,
  Peeping through the lock,
Are the children all in bed?
  For now it's eight o'clock!

Boys and girls come out to play,
The moon doth shine as bright as day.
Leave your supper and leave your sleep,
And join your playfellows in the street.
Come with a whoop and come with a call,
Come with a good will or not at all.
Up the ladder and down the wall,
A halfpenny loaf will serve us all.
You find milk and I'll find flour,
And we'll have pudding in half an hour.

80

Hey, diddle, diddle,

The cat and the fiddle,

The COW jumped over the moon.

The little dog laughed to see such sport,

And the dish ran away with the spoon.

Star light, star bright,
First **star** I see tonight,

I wish I may, I wish I might,
Have the **wish** I wish tonight.

Row, row, row your boat,
Gently down the stream.

Merrily, merrily, merrily, merrily,
Life is but a dream.

Twinkle, twinkle,
little star,
How I wonder
what you are.
Up above the
world so high,
Like a diamond
in the sky.

89

The man in the moon
Looked out of the moon,
Looked out of the moon and said,
"It's time, I think, for all good children
To think about going to bed."

Index of titles and first lines

Baa, baa, black sheep 54

Boys and girls come out to play 80

Cobbler, cobbler, mend my shoe 52

Cock robin got up early 6

Dickory, dickory, dare 58

Do your ears hang low? 26

Down by the station 48

Elsie Marley 8

Elsie put the kettle on 70

Here's a cup 72

Hey, diddle, diddle 83

Hickory, dickory, dock 22

Higglety, pigglety, pop 28

I can tie my shoelaces 10

I'm a little teapot 73

I saw you in the orchard 76

Jack and Jill 68

Jack be nimble 20

Little Bo-Peep 64

Little boy blue 62

Little Fee Wee 60

Little Miss Muffet 50

Mix a pancake 18

Oh where, oh where has my little dog gone... 39

One, two, buckle my shoe 36

Pat-a-cake 16

Pease porridge hot 14

Rain on the green grass 13

Rain, rain, go away.. 32

Rock-a-bye baby.. 40

Round about 30

Round and round the garden 44

Row, row, row your boat................................. 86

Star light, star bright 84

Teddy bear, teddy bear 45

The eensy weensy spider 34

The hen's in the house..................................... 66

The man in the moon 91

This little cow eats grass 42

To market, to market....................................... 56

Twinkle, twinkle, little star 89

Two little dicky birds 46

Wee Willie Winkie 78

Who made the pie?.. 74

Wiggle fingers, wiggle so 24

For Blair, Max and Brooke,
and you know why – H.C.

Kids Can Press acknowledges the financial support of the Government of Ontario,
through the Ontario Media Development Corporation's Ontario Book Initiative;
the Ontario Arts Council; the Canada Council for the Arts; and the
Government of Canada, through the BPIDP, for our publishing activity.

Published in Canada by
Kids Can Press Ltd.
29 Birch Avenue
Toronto, ON M4V 1E2

Published in the U.S. by
Kids Can Press Ltd.
2250 Military Road
Tonawanda, NY 14150

www.kidscanpress.com

The artwork in this book was rendered in watercolor.
The text is set in Joanna.

Edited by Jennifer Stokes and Yvette Ghione
Designed by Karen Powers
Printed and bound in China

This book is smyth sewn casebound.

CM 07 0 9 8 7 6 5 4 3 2

Library and Archives Canada Cataloguing in Publication

Out came the sun : a day in nursery rhymes /
illustrated by Heather Collins.

ISBN 978-1-55337-881-5 (bound)

1. Nursery rhymes. I. Collins, Heather

PZ8.3.O775 2007   j398.8   C2006-906849-6

Kids Can Press is a *Corus*™ Entertainment company